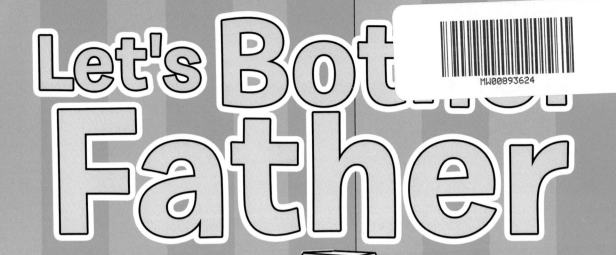

Let's Bother Father

Illustrated by
Frances Espanol

Richard D. Colton

To order additional copies of this book, contact:
Xlibris
1-888-795-4274
www.Xlibris.com
Orders@Xlibris.com

ISBN: 978-1-7960-8349-1 (sc)
ISBN: 978-1-7960-8348-4 (e)

Print information available on the last page

Rev. date: 01/16/2020

LET'S BOTHER FATHER

Richard D. Colton

It's Summer vacation!
Put the iPads away.
We have nothing to do
But go out and play.
Or, if we want to,
we can sleep all day.
But on this morning
I was first out of bed.
Ran to my brothers' rooms
and I said,
"Get up, you two,
vacation's begun!

It's time to go crazy!
It's time to have fun!"
But they both pulled the covers
back over their faces,
and mumbled they'd rather
just stay in their places.
Now this did not seem
to be like them at all,
not wanting to skateboard
or shoot basketball.

So I asked in surprise,
"What's wrong with you two?
Why stay inside when
there's so much to do?"
Then Paul said, "Richard,
you're out of your mind.
Just go to the window,
and peek out the blind."

Outside the sky was
as gray as could be.
The wind was howling
and bending the trees.
I said, "Looks to me like
there's a storm on the way."
Jeff said, "That's why, Genius,
we won't go out to play."

'Let's go to Mother," said Paul,
"and tell her we're bored."
"Why, so she can make us do chores?"
said Jeff (who always wound up
mopping the floor.)
"Okay, not her," I said,
"Where is Dad, then?"
Paul said, "He's working on-line
down in the den.
Been locked up in there
since way before ten."

"Brothers," I said, "forget
the rain and the chores.
I have an idea, and
we've done it before.
We're stuck in the house
But we still have a choice."
Then we smiled at each other
and we said with one voice,
"LET'S BOTHER FATHER!"

I said, "Okay, we have something now.
But we have to sit down
and figure out how.
'Cause if we're to bother him
as much as we can,
then we should get together
and come up with a plan."

So we thought for a while and then Jeff said, "Hey! Let's knock on the door then just run away."

"Too simple," Paul said, "And it might turn out bad. We just want to bother him, and not make him mad.

We could send him a text
that just says 'Duuuuuude.'
One message each minute
till he comes unglued!"
I said, "You two call him
somewhere else in the house.
I'll sneak into the den
and I'll unplug his mouse."

"I've heard enough," Dad said,
"I don't need to hear more.
(And we jumped when we saw him
right there in the door!)
"Who's up for a movie,
or a pizza buffet?
You boys shouldn't waste
your Summer this way.
Go get your Mom.
We'll do something together.
The car roof doesn't leak,
so don't mind the weather.

Get out of pajamas and into some jeans.
There's fun to be had,
if you know what I mean.
It's Summer vacation so
let's act like we care.
Get your windbreakers on,
and I'll meet you downstairs."
We felt like the happiest
three boys alive
as Dad backed the SUV
down the drive.
Because it was clear
to me, Jeff and Paul
that because he *is* Father,
we're no bother at all!

Printed in the United States
By Bookmasters